A Note to Parents

DK READERS is a compelling programme for beginning readers, designed in conjunction with leading literacy experts, including Maureen Fernandes, B.Ed (Hons). Maureen has spent many years teaching literacy, both in the classroom and as a consultant in schools.

Beautiful illustrations and superb full-colour photographs combine with engaging, easy-to-read stories to offer a fresh approach to each subject in the series.

Each DK READER is guaranteed to capture a child's interest while developing his or her reading skills, general knowledge and love of reading.

The five levels of DK READERS are aimed at different reading abilities, enabling you to choose the books that are exactly right for your child:

Pre-level 1: Learning to read

Level 1: Beginning to read

Level 2: Beginning to read alone

Level 3: Reading alone

Level 4: Proficient readers

The 'normal' age at which a child begins to read can be anywhere from three to eight years old. Adult participation through the lower levels is very helpful for providing encouragement, discussing storylines and sounding out unfamiliar words.

No matter which level you select, you c
be sure that you are helping your child
learn to read, then read to learn!

D1392996

LONDON, NEW YORK, MUNICH,
MELBOURNE AND DELHI

For Dorling Kindersley
Project Editor Heather Scott
Designer Owen Bennett
Brand Manager Lisa Lanzarini
Publishing Manager Simon Beecroft
Category Publisher Alex Allan
Production Controller Nick Seston
Production Editor Sean Daly

For Lucasfilm
Executive Editor Jonathan W. Rinzler
Art Director Troy Alders
Keeper of the Holocron Leland Chee
Director of Publishing Carol Roeder

Reading Consultant
Maureen Fernandes

This book is dedicated to Linus Beecroft

First published in Great Britain in 2008 by
Dorling Kindersley Limited, 80 Strand,
London, WC2R 0RL

6 8 10 9 7

SD345 – 05/08
Copyright © 2008 Lucasfilm Ltd. and ™
Page design copyright © 2008 Dorling Kindersley Limited

Published in the USA by DK Publishing

A CIP catalogue record for this book
is available from the British Library

ISBN: 978-1-4053-3278-1

Colour reproduction by Alta Image, UK
Printed and bound by L-Rex, China

Discover more at
www.dk.com
www.starwars.com

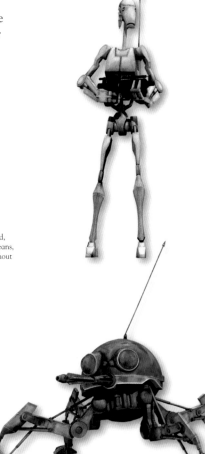

DK READERS

BEGINNING
TO READ ALONE
2

STAR WARS

THE CLONE WARS™

Anakin In Action!

Written by Simon Beecroft

A group of gunships fly through
the sky.
Each gunship carries soldiers
and Jedi generals.
The gunships are flying very fast.
They are on a dangerous mission.

Gunships
Gunships carry
soldiers into
battle.

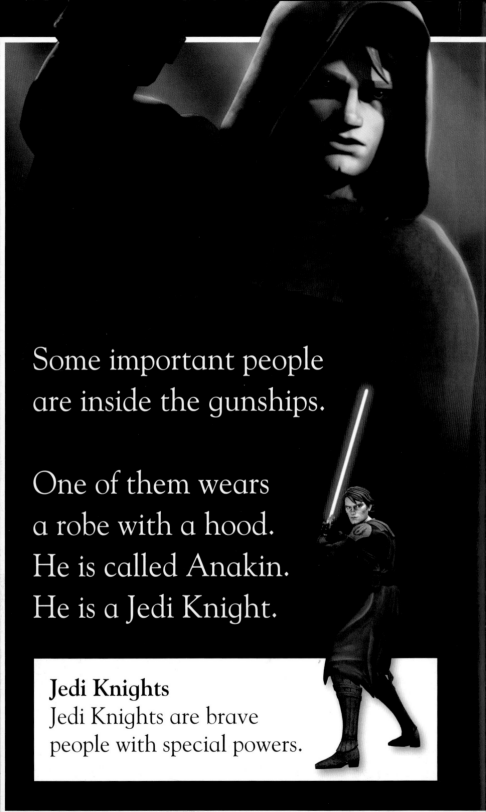

Some important people
are inside the gunships.

One of them wears
a robe with a hood.
He is called Anakin.
He is a Jedi Knight.

Jedi Knights
Jedi Knights are brave
people with special powers.

A soldier stands next to Anakin.
This soldier is Captain Rex.
Captain Rex wears a special
helmet over his face.
His body is protected by armour.

Another Jedi is travelling in
the gunship with Anakin.
Her name is Ahsoka.
Ahsoka is still learning her Jedi
powers. Anakin is her teacher.

Ahsoka has special
white patterns on her red skin.
She also has long head tails.

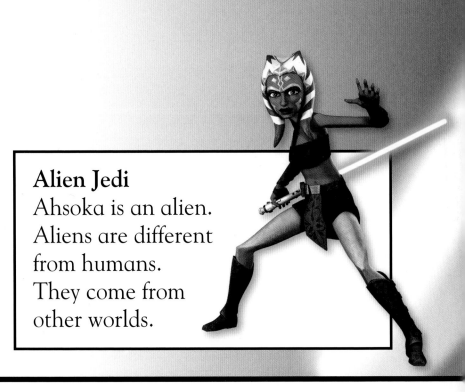

Alien Jedi
Ahsoka is an alien.
Aliens are different
from humans.
They come from
other worlds.

Anakin, Ahsoka and the clone
soldiers land close to a big castle.

They are going to rescue a young
creature called Rotta.
Rotta is a prisoner inside the castle.

Anakin is ready
with his lightsabre!

Clone soldiers
Clones are
humans who all
look and behave
the same way.

Enemy droids stand at the top of the castle wall. They see Anakin and the others land.

Spider droids have red eyes and walk on four mechanical legs. They start firing their big guns.

Battle droids also start firing.
Watch out Anakin!

Droid soldiers
Battle droids are not
human soldiers. They
are machine soldiers.

Anakin, Ahsoka and the clone
soldiers reach the castle wall.
It is so high they can hardly see
the top.
Captain Rex fires ropes out of his
blaster. The ropes hook onto the
top of the wall.

The Jedi and the soldiers all grab hold of the ropes and start climbing up. Anakin goes first and Ahsoka follows close behind. Clone soldiers in big tanks also start climbing the wall.

Clone tanks
These big tanks walk on six powerful legs. They can also climb walls.

Anakin has almost reached the top of the castle wall when battle droids on flying machines start to attack. Anakin thinks quickly.

He jumps onto one of the machines as it flies past.

STAPs
These flying machines are called STAPs. They have blaster cannons on the front.

Anakin kicks the droid off his flying machine.
Now he attacks the other droids!

After a lot of fighting, Anakin and Ahsoka reach the top of the castle wall.
They enter the castle.
The castle is cold and dark.

Baby Hutt
Rotta is a creature called a Hutt. Ahsoka carries him in a backpack.

Anakin and Ahsoka sneak along the creepy corridors.
Soon, they are able to find Rotta.
He is just a baby.
They must rescue Rotta quickly.
They must leave the castle quickly.

Too late! The droids
have blocked the exit.
Someone is with them.
This person looks dangerous.
She holds a lightsabre with
a red blade.

Her name is Ventress.
She has special powers like a Jedi.
Anakin, Ahsoka and Captain Rex
run back inside the castle
and lock the door.

Ventress breaks down the door to the castle. She goes inside to look for Anakin and Ahsoka.

In a dark room, Ventress finds Anakin and Ahsoka.
Anakin has nowhere to run.
He lights his blue lightsabre.
Ventress and Anakin fight each other with their lightsabres.
Clash!

Jedi enemy
Ventress uses a lightsabre like a Jedi. But she is not a Jedi. She is a deadly enemy of the Jedi.

Ahsoka is looking after Rotta. She is carrying him on her back. But she sees that Anakin needs her help.

Ahsoka jumps into the fight.
Ventress growls and
attacks Ahsoka.
Now all three of them
are fighting!

Ahsoka tries to find a way out of the dark room. She opens a heavy door. Big mistake!

A huge monstrous shape comes out of the shadows.
It is a rancor monster.

The rancor has sharp teeth and claws. It roars and attacks!

Rancors
Rancors are dangerous monsters with big heads and sharp claws and teeth.

Anakin and Ventress jump
onto the rancor's back
and continue fighting.
The rancor is confused.
It can no longer see Anakin
and Ventress.

Then the rancor
spots Ahsoka
and Rotta.

It moves toward them, as Anakin and Ventress fight on its back. Ahsoka stabs the rancor's foot.

It howls in pain and falls right on top of Ventress. Squish!

Anakin and Ahsoka think that the rancor has crushed Ventress. They escape from the castle with Rotta.

But after they have gone, there is a noise: vzzz!

It is a lightsabre being turned on.
Ventress is still alive!

Outside, Anakin tells Ahsoka
she was a great Jedi today.
A gunship arrives to take
them away. They are off
on another adventure!

Clone Wars Facts

Anakin Skywalker uses a lightsabre with a glowing blue blade.

Ahsoka uses a lightsabre with a green blade.

Ventress's lightsabres have red blades.

Captain Rex goes on missions with Anakin.

Rotta has thick, oily skin and orange eyes.